# I Heard Two Hippopotami

Written by
**Russel Hirst**

Illustrated by
**Airen Hall**

I heard **two hippopotami**
Conversing each with each;
They **wallowed** in the river
As I walked along the beach.

One **hippo** to the other said "You're **clumsy, slow,** and **fat.**

Your face is **very muddy,** and
Your forehead **low** and **flat.**

Your mouth is **huge** and **gaping**,
Belching noises **loud** and **hoarse**;

Your legs are **fat** and **baggy**,
Draped in skin both **thick** and **coarse**.

But . . .
The **hippo** who was talking
And was making all the fuss

Received **a loving smile** from
**Miss Hippopotamus.**

"Oh my!" she said,
"You flatterer!"
Then nuzzled on his shoulder.

The hippo **proves** that beauty's in
The eye of the beholder.

# About hippos

The name *hippopotamus* comes from two ancient Greek* words: *hippos* means *horse,* *potamus* means *river.* So: River Horse. Even though hippos may seem a bit like horses in the river, the animals most closely related to hippos are not horses but, surprisingly, whales and dolphins. Maybe that's why hippos love the water so much!

*Greek words made their way into English through other languages, like French. English has borrowed words from many languages—French, Spanish, Italian, etc. If you want to study the origins of words, you may want to study philology ("word loving") in school. Can you think of an English word that came from Spanish?

The hippo is the second-biggest land animal! Only elephants are bigger. The average female hippo weighs about 3,000 pounds, and the average male about 4,000 pounds (two tons), but since males keep growing all their lives, some can reach over *four* tons! How much do you weigh?

When there is more than one *hippopotamus,* we drop the "us" and change it to "i," which is the plural Latin* ending, making it *hippopotami.* This way of making a word plural is different from the way we make words plural from our English language heritage; we generally use an "s" or "es" at the end of the word—like in river/rivers, dog/dogs, or lunch/lunches. But because long ago English mixed with classical languages—Latin and Greek—some words we use in English still have Latin endings like "i."

*For example, the plural of *fungus* is *fungi*, and the plural of *cactus* is *cacti*. Still, some people these days are more comfortable making words plural in the English-heritage way. So it's fine if you want to say *cactuses* instead of cacti. You can even say *hippopotamuses* for more than one hippo, instead of *hippopotami* like in the poem. But isn't the word hippopotamus already long enough? Besides, you'll sound more like a scientist if you go with the Latin endings. Scientists love Latin.

But there's another option: we can shorten the word to *hippo* for one and *hippos* for more than one.

Hippos live in Africa and spend as long as 16 hours a day in the water. They can stay under water for up to five minutes. Hippos come out of the water at night to graze on nearby grasslands.

Hippos like to hang out in groups of about 10 to 30—called schools, dales, bloats, pods, or sieges. Watch a video of hippos running along together, and imagine they're heading towards your house! You'll understand why a group of them can be called a *siege*. (A siege is like an attack.)

Hippos are really loud, making a variety of snorts, grumbles, and wheezes. They are also considered very dangerous. They are not only enormous but also have huge teeth used for fighting.

But hippos just want their space; they don't want to eat you! They are herbivorous. That means they eat plants like grass, and fruit if they can find it. If needed, hippos can store grass in their stomachs for two days, and they can go three weeks without eating. How long can you go without eating?

# Words and phrases
# found in the poem

*They wallowed in the river*
**Wallow** is a verb often used when describing large mammals rolling and relaxing in mud or water. This activity keeps them cool and helps protect them from sunburns—and biting bugs!

*Belching noises loud and hoarse*
**Belching** means to make loud noises out of the mouth, caused by air coming up from the stomach. Ever had a burping contest with a friend?

*"Oh my!" she said, "You flatterer!"*
**Flatterer** is someone who says nice things to please or compliment another person, like the things the male hippo says in the poem. (But when you first heard the poem, did you think the male hippo was saying nice things?)

Sometimes the nice things said are true, but sometimes people say such things just to gain favor. In the poem, the lady hippo knows the gentleman hippo is sincere, so she appreciates his words and snuggles him. Remember, honesty is best! You can always find something good and true to say about others. Which brings us to the most important idea in the poem:

**Beauty is in the eye of the beholder.** To "behold" is to look at something with great attention. The whole phrase comes from an old saying meaning different people like different things. What seems unattractive to one person may be beautiful to another! For example, one person may love bugs—love to collect them, watch them, and read about them. Another person might run away from bugs.

Is there anything you like that your family or friends don't? It's nice that different people like different things. The world would be pretty boring if everybody liked exactly the same things.

*Beauty's in the eye of the beholder:* You get to decide the beauty of what you behold!

**Russel Hirst** has been a professor of English for several decades. He loves fishing and has spent a lot of time on mysterious and glorious rivers. Although he hasn't met any hippos in the wild, he has met all manner of river dwellers who speak to him.

The hippo conversation in the poem came to him many years ago as he lounged contentedly in front of a crackling wintertime fire, after a delicious superabundant feast at the beloved home of his youth in Northern California—the land of his awakening into semi-adult consciousness, where his mind has dwelt ever since.

**Airen Hall** is a writer and illustrator located in Washington, DC area. When she isn't making books and art, she is snuggling with her three cats or chasing after her two kids. You can see more of her work at https://withoutaladder.com/

 FriesenPress

Suite 300 - 990 Fort St
Victoria, BC, V8V 3K2
Canada

www.friesenpress.com

Illustrated by Airen Hall

ISBN
978-1-5255-9500-4 (Hardcover)
978-1-5255-9499-1 (Paperback)
978-1-5255-9501-1 (eBook)

*Juvenile Fiction, Animals, Hippos & Rhinos*

Distributed to the trade by The Ingram Book Company

CPSIA information can be obtained
at www.ICGtesting.com
Printed in the USA
BVHW021233050721
611165BV00005B/602